A NUMBER OF
ANIMALS

A NUMBER OF ANIMALS

STORY AND ILLUSTRATIONS BY

CHRISTOPHER WORMELL

WRITTEN BY KATE GREEN

CREATIVE EDITIONS

Text copyright © 1993 by Kate Green

Illustrations copyright © 1993 by Christopher Wormell

Designed by Ian Butterworth

Previous ISBN 978-1-56846-083-X

Previous LC Control No. 93-17134

This new edition published in 2012 by Creative Editions

P.O. Box 227, Mankato, MN 56002 USA

www.thecreativecompany.us

Creative Editions is an imprint of The Creative Company

Library of Congress Cataloging-in-Publication Data

Green, Kate.

A number of animals / written by Kate Green; illustrated by Christopher Wormell. — Rev. ed.

Summary: Introduces the numbers one through ten as a lost little chick

searches for its mother among groups of barnyard animals.

ISBN 978-1-56846-222-6

[1. Chickens—Fiction. 2. Domestic animals—Fiction.

3. Counting.] I. Wormell, Christopher, ill. II. Title.

PZ7.G82354Nu 2012   [E]—dc23   2011013229

CPSIA: 081111 PO1498

First Edition 9 8 7 6 5 4 3 2 1

For Daisy

I

Chick

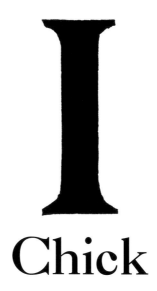

One little chick, lost and alone.

2
Horses

Two huge horses back by the stable.

"Have you seen my mother?"

"Not today," the horses neigh.

3
Cows

Three slow cows sunning in the meadow.

"Have you seen my mother?"

But all they do is moo.

Turkeys

Four fat turkeys ruffling their feathers.
"Gobble, gobble!" they gab
as they strut through the straw.

5
Goats

Five shaggy goats grazing in the field.
Their beards are hairy. Their horns are sharp.
"Baa-aa," they bleat. "No hens here!"

6

Geese

Six white geese waddling toward the water.

The little chick comes too close.

Look out!

7

Sheep

Seven sleepy sheep, woolly and warm.
The world is too big when you're all alone.

8
Ducks

Eight splashing ducks calling "quack, quack, quack."
The chick cheeps to them,
but the ducks don't quack back.

Pigs

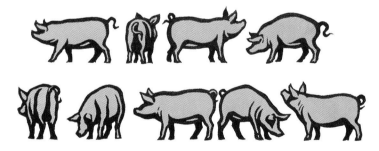

Nine pudgy pigs flopped in the mud.
"Wake up!" peeps the chick—
but what does he hear?

IO
Chicks

It's his sisters chirping and his brothers cheeping!
Now there are ten chicks ...

… and one mother hen!
"Here you are!" the little chick squeaks.
All ten chicks follow their mother home.

1 2 3 4 5

6 7 8 9 10